Inch by Inch

Leo Lionni

Alfred A. Knopf ⚘ New York

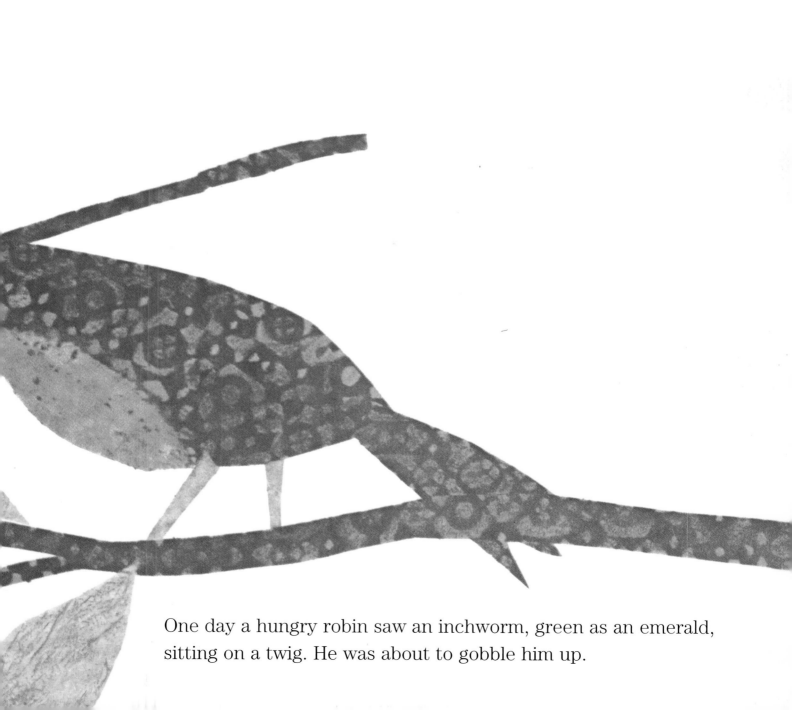

One day a hungry robin saw an inchworm, green as an emerald, sitting on a twig. He was about to gobble him up.

"Don't eat me. I am an inchworm. I am useful.
I measure things."
"Is that so!" said the robin. "Then measure my tail!"

"That's easy," said the inchworm.
"One, two, three, four, five inches."

"Just think," said the robin, "my tail is five inches long!"
And with the inchworm, he flew to where other birds needed to be measured.

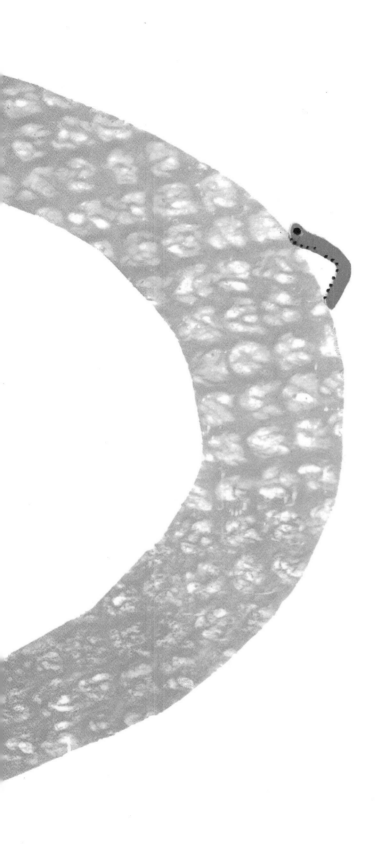

The inchworm measured the neck of the flamingo.

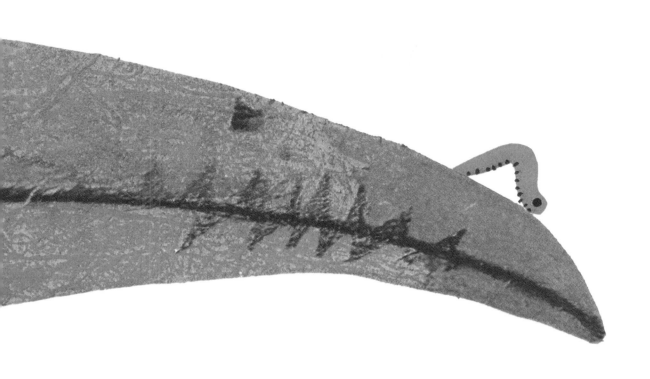

He measured the toucan's beak . . .

the legs of the heron . . .

the tail of the pheasant . . .

and the whole hummingbird.

One morning, the nightingale met the inchworm.

"Measure my song," said the nightingale.

"But how can I do that?" said the inchworm. "I measure things, not songs."

"Measure my song or I'll eat you for breakfast," said the nightingale.

Then the inchworm had an idea.

"I'll try," he said, "go ahead and sing."

The nightingale sang and the inchworm measured away.

He measured and measured . . .

Inch by Inch . . .

until he inched out of sight.

Leo Lionni, an internationally known designer, illustrator, and graphic artist, was born in Holland and studied in Italy until he came to the United States in 1939. He was the recipient of the 1984 American Institute of Graphic Arts Gold Medal and was honored posthumously in 2007 with the Society of Illustrators Lifetime Achievement Award. His picture books are distinguished by their enduring moral themes, graphic simplicity, and brilliant use of collage, and include four Caldecott Honor Books: *Inch by Inch, Frederick, Swimmy,* and *Alexander and the Wind-Up Mouse.* Hailed as "a master of the simple fable" by the *Chicago Tribune,* he died in 1999 at the age of 89.

THIS IS A BORZOI BOOK PUBLISHED BY ALFRED A. KNOPF

Copyright © 1960, renewed 1988 by Leo Lionni

All rights reserved. Published in the United States by Alfred A. Knopf, an imprint of Random House Children's Books, a division of Random House, Inc., New York. Originally published by McDowell, Obolensky, Inc., New York, in 1960. Reprinted by arrangement with Astor-Honor, Inc.

Knopf, Borzoi Books, and the colophon are registered trademarks of Random House, Inc.

Visit us on the Web! www.randomhouse.com/kids

Educators and librarians, for a variety of teaching tools, visit us at www.randomhouse.com/teachers

Library of Congress Cataloging-in-Publication Data
Lionni, Leo, 1910–1999.
Inch by inch / by Leo Lionni.
    p. cm.
Summary: To keep from being eaten, an inchworm measures a robin's tail, a flamingo's neck, a toucan's beak, a heron's legs, and a nightingale's song.
ISBN 978-0-375-85764-5 (trade) — ISBN 978-0-375-95764-2 (lib. bdg.)
[1. Caterpillars—Fiction. 2. Birds—Fiction.] I. Title.
PZ7.L6634Ip 2010
[E]—dc22
2009001767

The illustrations in this book were created using collage with colored pencil and crayon.

MANUFACTURED IN CHINA
April 2010
10 9 8 7 6 5 4 3 2 1
First Alfred A. Knopf Edition